Gabe & His Green Thumb

By David Mille

illustrated by
C.J.Love

© 2019 David Miller

ISBN- 978-0-578-52545-7

Printed in the United States

Learn more at daretobeking.net

For my Mom, Carol Christy Shelton Miller, my first teacher. I remember you teaching me how to grow tomatoes in our backyard.

Thanks to Derrick Barnes and Laurie Willis for editorial recommendations.

Special Thanks to C.J. Love for bringing Gabe to life!

16 Things Gabe likes doing in his garden

Planting Seeds

Putting his hands in the soil

Hunting for bugs

Watering vegetables

Pulling up weeds and dead leaves

Planting with his friends

Harvesting the vegetables

Digging in the garden

Learning "everything" gardening

Getting vegetables ready for the market

Talking about the garden

Finding worms

Taking pictures of the vegetables

Count the vegetables

Measure the vegetables

Making compost for fertilizer

Gabe and Alex have been cool since the first grade.

While scoring during a soccer game, Alex ran Gabe over one day at recess. But he helped Gabe up, they've been best buddies ever since.

Gabe has been gardening with his parents since he was old enough to walk. In his spare time, you can always find him in his backyard working in his own private garden. He loves it!

When he's not reading comics, Gabe spends most of his time in his garden.

"Dude, gardening is so lame," Alex said.

"Just try it once. You'll never be the same," Gabe replied.

"Who knows what'll happen if I stick my hand in that dirt? I'll pass," said Alex.

One day a strong storm swept through the area, which meant no soccer for Alex and no gardening for Gabe.

The sky opened up. Dark clouds covered every inch of the sky, and rain pounded the ground like thousands of tiny drumsticks. For two days it rained super hard, nonstop.

A few days later the dark clouds rolled away, and the skies were clear blue once again.

The sun slowly poked through the thin, white clouds.

Gabe put on his boots, overalls and played in the small puddles left from the storm.

He called Alex and asked him to come over to help out in the garden.

"C'mon, man. It won't take too long," begged Gabe.

"Okay. Twenty minutes. That's it," replied Alex.

Most of the ground was still wet, so the boys spent time pulling weeds, adding mulch and raking dirt.

Gabe saw a huge earthworm peek out from beneath the soil.

"Watch this!" he said to Alex as he shoved his hand deep into the soil. "Come on out, you slimy little fish bait."

"Can you feel him?" asked Alex.

"Nope----I think I do----OUCH!" yelled Gabe. "Feels like I stuck my thumb on a thorn or something bit me."

"But worms don't bite," replied Alex. "Let's see it."

When Gabe pulled his thumb out and looked at it, there wasn't a mark.

"Looks fine to me," said Alex.

"Feels fine too," said Gabe. "I'll be okay, but I'm going home. Later for this garden, buddy."

The next morning, Gabe woke up to the sound of his mother yelling at the top of her lungs from downstairs, "GET UP, GABE MANDELA GRESHAM! YOU DON'T WANT TO BE LATE FOR SCHOOL!"

Gabe jumped out of bed and rolled into the bathroom, still half asleep.

Gabe was so sleepy that he brushed his teeth with his eyes closed. But when he opened them he got the shock of his life!

"My thumb, my thumb," he hollered!

Gabe's parents raced into the bathroom.

"What's the problem, son?" his dad asked.

"Look at my hand. My thumb is big and green!" said Gabe.

"What happened to your hand," Gabe's dad asked.

"Does it hurt, honey?" asked his mom.

"It doesn't hurt, but it sure is big," Gabe replied.

"We are going to the doctor's office right now," said his mom.

So Gabe, his parents, Alex, and even Pharaoh, his Jack Russell Terrier all jumped in the car!

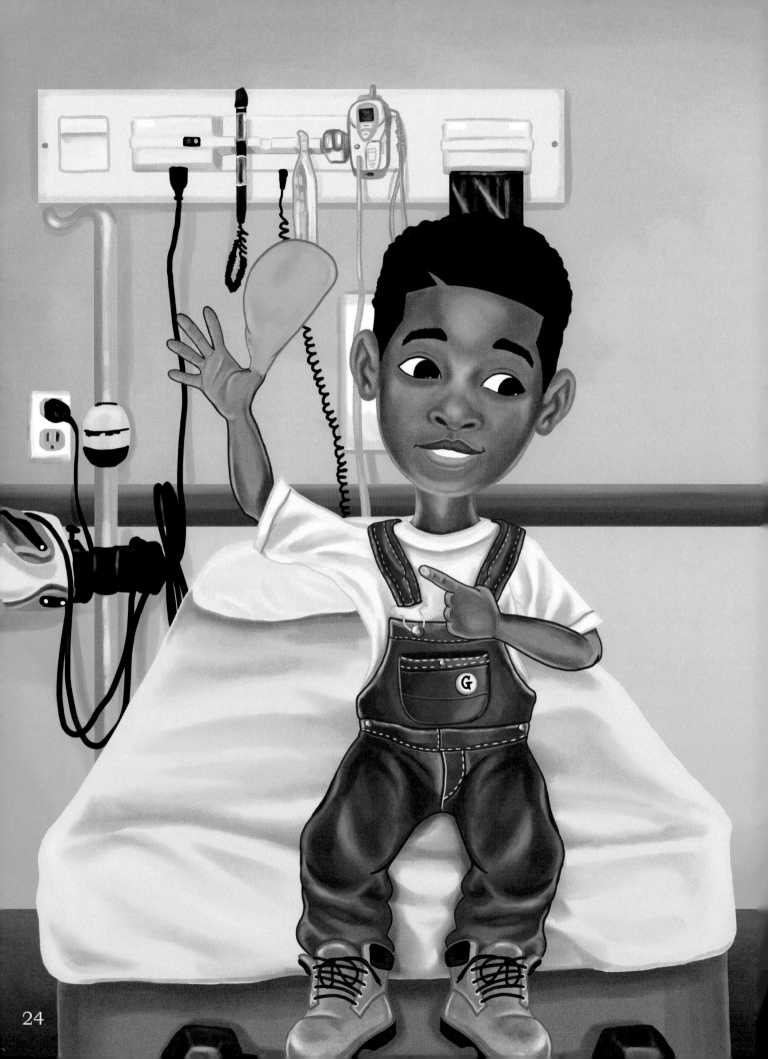

"How are you doing, Gabe?" asked Dr. McMichael.

"I am feeling okay, but look at my thumb," said Gabe.

"Whoa!" said Dr. McMichael "How'd that happen?"

"I don't know. I was messing around in my garden," said Gabe. "Woke up this morning---and now I have this."

He stuck out his thumb, and it was the size of a lime!

And it was getting even bigger!

"Never seen anything like it in my life," said Dr. McMichael. "Let's get an X-ray."

After the X-rays came back negative, with nothing broken, Gabe left with his parents.

His thumb was still green and now as big as an oversized avocado.

"Seeing how this is the first time I've seen anything like this, and all of your tests came back okay, all I can say is good luck with that. It should be fine sometime soon. I guess..." said Dr. McMichael as he shrugged his shoulders.

NEGATIVE
Normal

Gabe began to run off a bunch of questions to his parents. "Can I go to school? What will the kids say?

What will happen to my thumb? Will the green color go away?"

His parents just held both of his hands as they walked out of Dr. McMichael's office in silence.

The next day, Gabe dragged himself to school. He was teased and laughed at by kids in class for the first couple of days. Weeks passed. Then months passed. And Gabe's thumb was still big and green – but now it was the size of a small, juicy watermelon. The only person that didn't think Gabe's thumb was weird was his old buddy Alex.

"Man---that is some sight, Gabe. I wish I had it," said Alex

"I wish I could give it to you," said Gabe

"Come on over to the garden. Maybe sticking your hand back into the soil will reverse the swelling," said Alex

Gabe was desperate. He agreed.

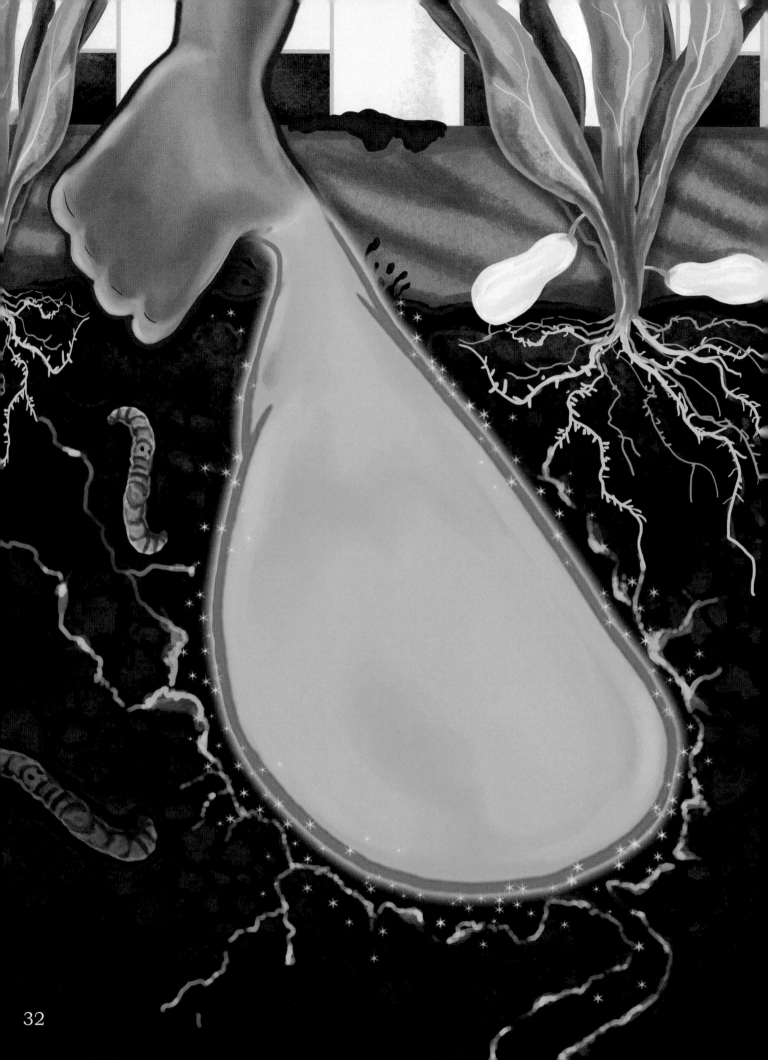

Gabe got down on his knees right between the row of green beans and the row of squash. He dug his hand into the same spot where he was reaching for the worm. All of a sudden, something magical started happening. The vegetables in each row started growing right before their eyes!

"Would you look at that! You've got a magical green thumb, Gabe Gresham!" yelled Alex.

At first Gabe was shocked, but he stuck his hand in a little deeper, which made the entire row of squash grow to their full size. It was amazing.

He was now the talk of Philadelphia. The boy with the big, magical green thumb.

From that moment on, Gabe and Alex loaded up a wheelbarrow with huge vegetables.

Bright red tomatoes were ten to fifteen pounds, monster sized cabbage were thirty pounds and onions were the size of basketballs.

Channel 6 news heard about the monster-sized vegetables Gabe was growing and sent a reporter to his house.

"What kinds of vegetables do your grow?" asked the reporter from Channel 6.

Gabe answered, "We grow kale, carrots, onions, tomatoes, peppers, cucumbers, and radishes."

THE KID WITH THE MAGICAL GREEN THUMB!

BREAKING NEWS

"We heard people in Philly call you the kid with the magical green thumb," the reporter said.

"Yes. I'm not sure what happened, but since my thumb turned green, whenever I stick my hand in the dirt magic happens," Gabe told the reporter.

NEWS 6

PHILLY NEWS   4:30   75°

▶ **GABE GRESHAM**

All kinds of super cool things were happening thanks to Gabe's green thumb. Two days ago, Gabe and his family drove to Allentown, Pennsylvania. There, Gabe presented his vegetables at the Pennsylvania State Fair.

At five thirty a.m., Gabe and his family loaded up the van and hit the road. Of course, Alex and Pharaoh jumped in the back. Pharaoh barked for the first twenty minutes of the trip. On the way, Gabe and Alex wrote down the names of the states on license plates that they saw while riding down the highway.

Mississippi, Michigan, Maryland, West Virginia, Illinois, Texas…Gabe must have counted about thirty states on the drive to Allentown.

44

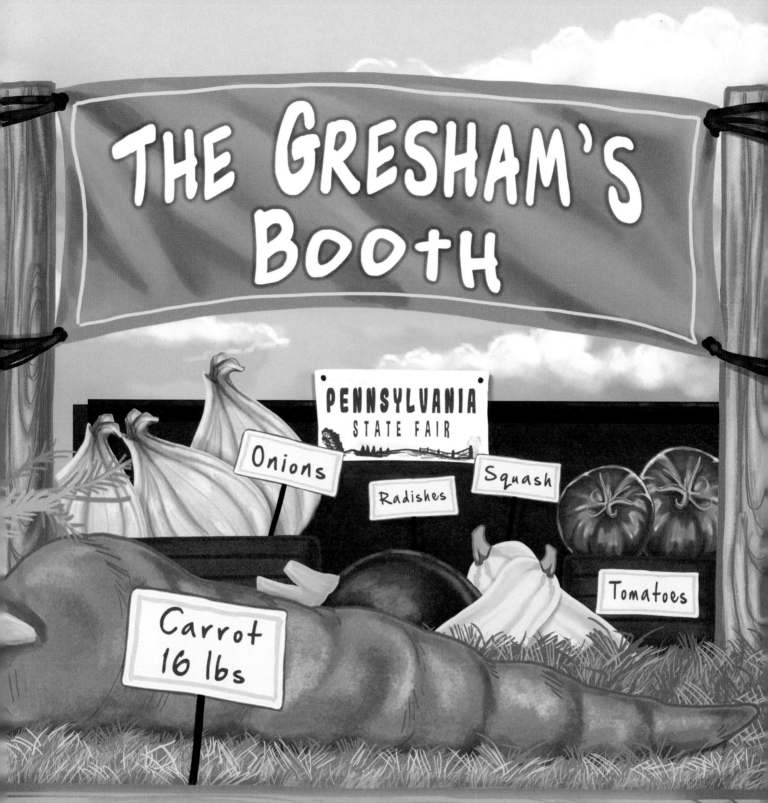

Gabe and his family arrived early at the State Fair to set up his booth. The Gresham's booth featured tomatoes, radishes, onions and carrots. Once they finished setting up their booth, Gabe and his family spent time walking around looking at animals and farm equipment.

The judging would take a while. The judges were looking at the size, weight and color of the vegetables.

After a few hours, the judges walked on stage and grabbed the mic.

"The winner for first place, with a carrot weighing sixteen pounds---- Gabe Gresham from Philadelphia!" the older man on stage announced.

Gabe became the youngest person in the history of the Pennsylvania State Fair to win a Blue Ribbon – for his sixteen-pound carrot.

Gabe's mom was so excited she almost knocked him down while jumping up and down when his name was called.

"See, didn't I tell you that gardening was cool?" Gabe and Alex laughed.

Gabe walked on stage with his parents and Pharaoh, sporting a smile that could be seen across the state of Pennsylvania. The judges handed Gabe a Blue Ribbon and a large check for five hundred dollars.

Pay To The Order Of

GABE GRESHAM

1ST PLACE

WINNER!

When Gabe returned home the next day, he was running late for school as usual. When he got to his classroom ten minutes late, he peeked his head in the door and saw his teacher, Ms. Gilbert, holding up the newspaper so the class could see a big photo of him, his parents, Alex and Pharaoh at the State Fair.

Then Ms. Gilbert turned the page to show the class another photo with Gabe and his parents holding his prized Blue Ribbon for First Place.

"Your classmate, Gabe Gresham, won 'BIG' at the Pennsylvania County Fair with a carrot that he grew in his backyard."

Gabe finally stepped into the room, with his big green thumb behind his back. He expected to be in trouble for being late again and for his classmates to laugh at him and his freakishly big green thumb just as they have for weeks.

But this time, they all stood to their feet and cheered, "GABE-GABE-GABE-GABE!"

And just like that, Gabe became one of the coolest kids in school.

Nowadays, Gabe's thumb is still big and green.

Drive by the Gresham house any afternoon after school, and you will find plenty of neighborhood kids in the garden with Gabe, Alex and of course, Pharaoh.

Gabe's top suggestions for what to grow in a vegetable garden:

a. Beets
b. Carrots
c. Cucumbers
d. Eggplant
e. Green Beans
f. Lettuce
g. Kohlrabi
h. Muskmelon
I. Onions
j. Peppers
k. Potatoes
l. Radishes
m. Shallots
n. Spinach
o. Squash
p. Swiss Chard
q. Tomatoes
r. Cabbage

David Miller is the author of several books, including the Greene Family Farm and Khalil's Way. Miller's work with youth has been featured in the *BBC Magazine, Huffington Post* and on *NPR, PBS* and *CNN*.
He enjoys cooking, fishing and reading in front of the fireplace.
David lives in Washington, DC with his wife and children.
Visit David's work at www.daretobeking.net

About the Illustrator:
C.J. Love is a graduate of Maryland Institute College of Art,
with a Bachelor of Fine Arts in Graphic Design. He specializes
in illustration, caricatures, mural painting, graphic design, and
prototype designs.

Made in the USA
Middletown, DE
14 February 2020